Quick, Slick & Longing To Lick

The Complete Series — Books 1-6

Steph Brothers

Contents

Blurb

These kitties are *all about* curiosity...

Married, single, or in between...every girl needs some girl-time.

Whether they're giving or receiving, experienced or innocent, being pampered or being punished, these women waste no time getting down to the business of pleasure.

Never send a boy to do a girl's job.

My Masseuse

LAST NIGHT, I FINALLY broke up with Tim. We had a good few months, but lately he'd been making those kinds of remarks. *Why don't you go blonde? Maybe you could afford to lose a few pounds.*

Well, I like my hair brunette, but it turned out shifting the weight was easy. I lost 200 useless pounds with one quick decision.

But now, it was Tuesday morning and I was exactly where I needed to be. In my masseuse's studio, for my weekly session, face down and naked. Just a towel over my lower half.

I glanced up as I heard the door open.

"Hi, Grace," said Zoe as she breezed in, wearing her emerald-colored silk robe that somehow worked perfectly with her fiery red hair. I cast an envious eye over her gorgeous body. That robe really highlighted her shapely breasts and round hips. "How are you today?"

I sighed, and left it at that.

"Aha," she replied. "So, I'm guessing that means Tim is out of the picture now?"

"Yes, thank fuck."

"Well, then I'll simply have to make you forget all about him."

"Fine by me. And if you can make me forget all other men, too, that'd be awesome."

"You sure you want to do *that*, honey?"

"Ugh. Absolutely. Men are just too much trouble. At least for now."

Zoe chuckled, and picked up her heated oil. "Then I can do that for you. And that's *no* trouble."

She poured the warm, syrupy liquid on my lower back and I hummed with delight. Not just for the exquisite way it felt, but because it was the signal that I'd be feeling a whole lot better, really soon. Everywhere on my body.

"Before I completely wipe your memory, did you want to talk about it?"

"Oh, there's not much to say." I stopped talking as Zoe coaxed a low moan out of me. "He was trying to change me and I just didn't need that."

"Change you? In what way? Is he crazy?"

"Mmm...apparently I'm not a skinny blonde."

"Huh. Well of course you're not. You're a beautiful, curvaceous brunette that *anyone* would be glad to be with."

Zoe truly had magic hands, and as she spread the oil over the length and breadth of my back, she pressed her short-nailed fingers into my flesh.

"Oh, god," I moaned. "That's so good, I've already forgotten his name."

"Can you still picture his face?"

"Yeah."

Zoe leaned down close to my ear. "Then buckle up, honey. Time to unleash the big guns."

She stood at the top of the massage table, and with my face in the head-hole, all I could see was her long, shapely legs. I glanced down at her pretty feet, bare as always, with funky blue and gold polish on her nails.

Pretty soon, she was coaxing small—and big—moans from me with her fingers, thumbs and palms. Pressing them into my back, working the tension out of my body. I closed my eyes and let Zoe's skillful touch take me to the heights of relaxation and pleasure.

She moved around to the side of the table and broke contact for a second. I heard a slight rustling sound, and then two hard points of pressure dug into my back.

"I remember how you like my elbows," Zoe said, her voice calm and soothing.

"Mmm..." Oh, god. I was moaning more than I ever did in bed with...*whatshisname*. That was the power Zoe had over me. In the two years I'd been coming to her, she'd given me more pleasure than all my boyfriends combined.

Once she'd broken down the knots in my shoulders, she switched back to hands, and swept them wide, from my neck to my waist.

I caught my breath as she glided one hand down and under the top of my towel, but she slid back out right away.

The next long glide, though, had her pressing right down, cupping the bare cheek of my ass. She gave it a good squeeze, and then released.

"Uh..." I wasn't sure what she was doing. All I knew was, it felt...good. *Better* than good.

Zoe leaned up to my ear again. "How are we doing, Grace? Can you still picture him?"

"Umm...m-maybe." Honestly, at that moment I was having trouble picturing the floor I was staring at. I wasn't sure exactly what Zoe was planning. I wasn't sure what I was prepared to have done to me.

But she'd never steered me wrong before. It was almost as if she could read my mind, sometimes, the way she worked my muscles and limbs over.

"Well, if you still remember him, then I haven't done my job yet. Have I, Grace?"

"Um...no."

Zoe eased around to the foot of the table, and took hold of my towel. "We're going to have to lose this."

"Oh, uh...do we have to?" It seemed like a huge step, to be bare-assed in a semi-public place and all.

"Yeah, we do, Grace."

Before I could even take another breath, she pulled my towel off.

I was utterly naked, with my masseuse at my feet. Oh, god, what must she be able to see of me from that angle? I clamped my legs together.

"Hey, uh, Zoe..."

"Shh. You said you wanted to forget all men."

"Y-yeah. I guess."

"And what do you think it would take to make that happen, honey?"

I hadn't even tried to put it into words. It wasn't even a serious request really. Just a snappy one-liner that jumped into my mind just before it jumped into my mouth.

"Well," Zoe continued. "Do you think me giving you multiple orgasms might work?"

"Ohh..." I'd never been with another woman. I'd never really thought about it, except in passing. If I had to choose a woman to take my girl-cherry, though, Zoe would definitely be the one.

My mind turned mushy at the thought of the ecstasy a woman might give me. I knew instinctively where to touch myself when I needed pleasure. There was every chance this gorgeous masseuse would, too. After all, she had the same bits I did, and was trained the art of sensual touching. I was just a clumsy—but enthusiastic—amateur.

Zoe poured warm oil up and down the lengths of my legs, and goosebumps rose across my body. I couldn't do this, could I? Let a woman touch me in...my untouchables?

The moment she pushed her soft hands up from my ankle to my thigh, though, I was hers.

She clambered up onto the table behind me, straddling my legs as she squeezed and released the muscles of my thigh.

She crept her deft fingers higher, ever higher, and I licked my lips in anticipation.

The sweet tingling of arousal erupted in my pussy as Zoe worked her thumbs into the meat of my ass. She slid her hand across the crease where butt meets thigh, and suddenly I found it hard to breathe.

Slowly, Zoe eased her hands to the other side and worked it over. Damn, it was good. Not too hard, and not too soft. Just...*perfect.*

I felt her weight shift, and then the bare skin of her knee pressed down between my legs. After barely a second of hesitation, I spread my thighs to let her in.

"Good girl," Zoe said. For some reason that little bit of praise made the hair on the back of my neck tingle. It was just so...*sweet.*

All the guys I'd been with were blunt and basic. *Fuck, yeah. Suck it, bitch.* Sometimes that was just what I needed. Right now, though...Zoe's soft words matched her touch so perfectly.

She broke through my wandering thoughts, gliding her oily hands up both of my legs. She had her thumbs dug right into the sensitive skin of my inner thighs, and I whimpered with need as she came closer to home.

And then, she was there, her thumbs pressed to my outer lips. When she moved them both in small circles, I let out a breathy moan.

Having my masseuse touch me like that was so much better than touching myself. She glided one hand up and rested it on my lower back, making random patterns.

But her other hand she kept down there, where the action was. She pressed her thumb to my clit and I bucked like I'd been shot.

"Oh, fuck...Zoe..."

"Mm. You smell wonderful, Grace."

"Uhh..."

She spun her hand, bringing her fingers to my pleasure bud and making tight circles. I pulled my legs wide apart and arched my back, raising my hips off the table. And I did it all without a single thought.

"Oh..." Zoe said, her voice going soft. "Your pussy is just so pretty. I can't wait to kiss her."

"Oh, *ffffuck...*" I truly had never imagined I'd do anything with a woman. But suddenly, the idea of this gorgeous creature putting her mouth on me—anywhere at all—was my life's goal. And she was making good on her promise, too. The only thoughts I had about men was how poorly I'd chosen them.

I jumped in surprise when she pressed the tip of her thumb to my ass hole. *No-man's-land*, as I thought of it. I'd never let any guy touch me there, let alone put anything into it.

But with Zoe teasing my clit so perfectly, the sensation of her tickling my ass as well made the moment whole.

I bit my lip and rolled over onto my back. I wasn't at all surprised to see Zoe had stripped off her robe and was completely naked. That was probably the rustling I heard before she dug her elbows into my back.

Her body was even sexier than I'd thought it would be. Smooth pale skin that looked as edible as ice cream. Pretty pink nipples that were begging for my mouth.

Holy hell. Not only was I suddenly into women...clearly, I was a bit of a slut about it.

Zoe glided her beautiful body forward and took my mouth in a sensual kiss. Her lips were softer than any I'd kissed before, but below the surface she was a ravenous beast.

She drove her tongue into me, and I was powerless to resist. The wonderful sensation of her big, soft breasts rubbing against mine lit a fresh new fire inside me. One more reminder that I was going somewhere I'd never gone before.

I took a handful of Zoe's lush hair and slid my tongue past hers, exploring her mouth as if I'd lost something there. Like my sanity, maybe. Zoe moaned in delight and ground her talented hand against my sopping wet slit.

When she hooked two fingers and drove them inside me, my moans turned to wails.

Zoe grabbed my breast and kneaded it, grinding the flesh against my body as she eased her mouth away from mine. I snared her tongue between my teeth, not ready to stop kissing her. After all, I'd only just found out how fucking incredible it could be.

When she squeezed my nipple between her thumb and finger, though, I yelped with the beautiful pain of it, and she escaped.

Before I could make another sound, she sank her teeth into my throat, and twisted my nipple, all while pumping her long fingers in and out of my cunt.

And when she pressed her thumb to my clit again, I was in fucking heaven. No man had ever treated me so well. Zoe was doing to me everything I'd do to myself, if only I had extra hands and a spare mouth.

My sexy masseuse seemed to know exactly what I needed, every moment. She released her bite and gave my neck a light kiss, then slid the tip of her tongue down to my nipple.

The heat of her mouth was amazing as she engulfed my stiff bud. Every pull of her sweet lips and tongue drew tingling pleasure up from deep inside me.

"Zoe...that's so nice..."

"I can't wait any longer. I have to taste you."

"Ohh..."

She slid herself back and put her feet on the floor, pulling me along with her. For a few moments, she stroked the waxed-bare skin of my mound, a sweet little smile curling her pretty mouth. When she hooked her hands around my thighs I held my breath.

Zoe bent in close to my wanton slit and drew in a long breath. "God, you smell so fucking good."

"Th-thank you."

Zoe looked deep into my eyes. "I've wanted to do this for so long, Grace."

She smiled straight at me, turning the moment just a little more tender. Then she raised her eyebrows and licked her lips, and I melted.

When Zoe pressed her hot tongue to my wet slit, I bucked my hips like crazy. Maybe it was the buildup, or maybe she really had some magic skills. Either way, I'd never reacted so strongly to a tongue on my pussy.

Slowly, she dragged her wet muscle up the length of my slit. When she reached the tip she drew her tongue back into her mouth, closing her eyes and savoring my juices.

"Wow. You taste even better than I imagined, honey."

Before I could reply, she fell on me again, driving her firm tongue against my slick lips, awakening in me a new level of pleasure.

Zoe mewed like a wildcat, clawing at my thighs so hard she managed to scratch me, even with those short nails. She explored every pore of my pussy, and up and down the lengths of my inner thighs.

I took hold of her gorgeous red hair and made tight fists.

"Mmm..." Zoe hummed, her sweet voice vibrating against my juicy cunt. "Harder, honey."

I pulled my knees up and spread my thighs as wide as I could. As I dragged on Zoe's hair, I rolled my hips, marking her whole face with my scent. Declaring that she was mine, at least for now.

Zoe snarled as she bit, lick and sucked at my most tender flesh. She pushed forward, driving her tongue deep into my cunt and moaning with need.

I arched my back as I felt a climax coming on, and Zoe slid her hands up my body. She grabbed my tits and pummeled them as she planted her hot mouth over my clit.

The moment her wet heat engulfed my pleasure bud, I knew I was past the point of no return. She flicked it with her tongue and the first tingles of orgasm awoke inside me.

But when she sucked hard, pulling my stiff little clit to life as she pinched my nipples, my belly erupted in a wildfire of ecstasy. Glittering fingers of pure bliss swept through my body, out to my fingers and toes and back into my core.

As my climax eased, and I managed to get my breath back, I released my grip on Zoe's hair.

"Holy fuck," I said, barely managing to get my voice past a whisper.

Zoe clambered up on the table again and for the first time I could properly see her pretty waxed pussy. She crawled forward until her face was above mine, and she smiled.

I put my hands around the back of her neck and pulled her down for a deep kiss, gliding my tongue into her mouth and exploring the way my juices tasted on her skin.

Her sweet moans were like music, and I knew I needed more. I needed to make her truly sing.

I pulled my lips away from hers and she stroked my hair. Maybe she thought we were done, but I had better ideas.

I shimmied part way down the table, stopping when my face bumped against Zoe's beautiful round breasts.

Nervousness crept into my mind for a second as I reached up and pressed those bountiful mounds together. Zoe simply sighed, and my nerves disappeared.

Working on instinct only, I pulled her nipple into my mouth and caressed it with my tongue. Zoe moaned and angled herself, pressing more of her velvet flesh against my face.

"That's so nice, Grace. You're very good at that."

Her praise put me even further at ease, and I decided to go for broke.

Inching my way further down, I kissed Zoe's soft, beautiful belly. But I couldn't move any further without leaving my ass hanging off the foot of the table.

"Come up to meet me, Zoe."

"Wh-what?"

"I want to taste you. Make you feel as wonderful as you made me feel."

"Y-you don't have to. I mean, *I'm* the masseuse. You're the *client*."

"I really want to. More than I've wanted anything in a long time."

Zoe sighed, closing her eyes with a smile. "Yes..."

She inched her way forward, bringing that sweet, fragrant flower of hers closer to me.

Her scent was so similar to mine, but with a slight twist. I wasn't sure if I should be scared, but at that moment all I felt was anticipation.

Slowly, I raised my head and planted a soft, closed-mouth kiss against the fiery heat of Zoe's slit. I came away again with a delicious, sticky sound that had my belly tensing with want.

As Zoe gazed down at me, her big blue eyes wide open with desire, I licked my lips. The taste of my masseuse's arousal was spicy and fresh, and made me even hungrier for her.

I snared her pretty thighs in my hands and pulled, dragging her down as I raised my head. Without even meaning to, I let out a snarling, lioness sound just as I planted my open mouth against her slick lips.

Zoe bucked her hips forward and back as I made circles with my head, exploring every part of her juicy slit. I worked my tongue as deep inside her as I could, searching for any part of her I might have missed.

A new burst of sparkling desire formed in my core and I slid my hand down, grinding my fingers against my clit as I lapped at my masseuse's hot pussy.

Zoe fell forward, driving her clit against my tongue, then rolled her hips. The way she took control, even when it was my mouth doing the pleasuring, made the moment even more special. In truth, I hadn't been confident I could eat pussy at all, but like this, with Zoe in charge, it let me lie back and be her sex toy.

She took a handful of my hair and dragged, pulling my face against her sweet cunt and pumping at me. It was the most erotic moment of my life to watch her as she gave herself over to the climax rising inside her.

I always knew Zoe was a free spirit, but to see the unashamed way she rode her orgasm, let it take her body over, let it paint expressions of pained pleasure on her beautiful face...it was almost a religious experience for me.

With one final burst, Zoe mashed her fragrant pussy into my mouth and let out a long, keening cry of ultimate pleasure. I pinched my clit in harmony and my own climax fired through me. We came together like some beautiful carnal ballet.

As Zoe's pulsing body gradually slowed, I eased my mouth off her, peppering her tender flesh with light kisses, from thigh to thigh and everywhere in between.

She scooted backward, and slowly, like molasses dripping, brought her pretty mouth down to take me in a kiss made even more delicious by our shared juices.

Zoe moaned against my tongue and eased herself lower and lower, kissing my neck, my breasts and my belly as she worked her way back down off the foot of the table.

She stopped, and took my pussy in a deep, soft kiss, one last time before she stood.

"Well?" she asked, with a cheeky grin.

"Hmm?"

"Did I make you forget?"

I slid myself down off the table, struggling to stand on my mushy legs. "Zoe, I can't even remember what I was trying to forget. That was...awesome."

"I'm so glad. Same time next week?"

"Now *that*, I'll remember."

THE END

Derby Domination

I WAS STILL NEW to Roller Derby, but it was fast becoming everything to me. It's the one thing I didn't have to share with my boyfriend, Neil. He doesn't come to watch, he doesn't even bring me. I power it all.

Derby's my one chance to be a boy. I mean, I'm a girly-girl through and through, and I love being soft and feminine. Heck, with a name like Poppy, what choice did I have? I've always been the short one, the pretty one, the one with the tiny voice that turns into a screech if I shout.

All Neil has to do is stand up and speak, and people take him seriously. It helps that he's 6'3" in socks. I'm only 5'3" in stilettos.

But I'm 5'4" in skates. And when I'm in uniform, I inhabit the persona of *Poppy Speeds, jammer extraordinaire*. Even my voice transforms from screech to siren.

This particular night had been amazing. My team, Nymph Formation, had taken the victory against the Maulrats. Why that was so important to me was because of one particular blocker on the other team. More than anything else I loved teasing the hell out of her.

Her real name was Alex, but on the track, she called herself Di Screaming. Tall, blonde, and fierce, when she was in full flight she was a glorious Valkyrie. And she was officially my girl-crush.

Didn't matter she sneered at me every time our teams met. That I hadn't ever spoken a word to her, except on the track. She was bursting with charisma, and could probably carry me under her arm if she chose to.

Seriously, she was nearly as tall as my boyfriend, and though she was curvy as hell, I'd seen her getting changed. Those big thighs were all muscle. Her abs could massage my back on their own. Her arms were more toned and muscular than Neil's.

During post-match drinks, I watched Alex as she chugged a second beer. There was nothing subtle about her at all. She'd be loud, even in a coma. She's just built that way.

With a long gulp, she swallowed the last of her beer and slammed the bottle onto the table. Then she stared across at me like I'd called her fat or something. It was more than disturbing. It was actually frightening. As much for the anger in her eyes as for the tingle it sent firing down my spine.

Sure, I'd given her hell throughout the match, but she must have known that was all for the show. She'd been doing this way longer than I had. I tried a coquettish smile as a peace offering, the type I use on Neil all the time.

Her only reply was to raise her hand in the shape of a gun and mime shooting me. I waited for her to smile back, to prove she was joking, but there was nothing.

On the track, I was a beast. They call it white line fever in football. But out of uniform and back in civvies, there was no way I was up for any kind of confrontation, especially with a girl as big and strong as Alex. I quickly sucked up the last of my drink and made my excuses to the girls.

My helmet felt like it was made from stone as I picked it up to head out of the arena. I knew Alex's eyes were boring a hole in the back of my head as I tripped across the wooden floor. Why didn't I wear sensible clothes, like jeans and joggers, instead of my tight T, short skirt and oh-so-pretty heels? At least I had my riding jacket.

Though I'd parked my scooter pretty close to the arena, the alleyway was poorly lit at this time of night. The wind had picked up a little and rattled the dumpster lids. I thought I heard something else—maybe a cat mewing—but I wasn't sure.

As I reached my scooter, I glanced back over my shoulder. And then froze with my helmet halfway up to my head. She was there, ten feet away at the mouth of the alley. Di Screaming.

I mean, it was Alex, but I couldn't see her as anything but the fierce monster she was on track.

She had her hands in the pockets of her knee-length leather coat and she looked as imposing as any man would. The light was behind her and I couldn't see her face, but my imagination pasted a very angry look on it.

I admit it. I panicked. There was no time to even start my scooter, let alone turn and ride away. Instinct took over from thought.

I dropped my helmet and bag, spun around and ran as fast as my heels would let me.

Even over the gusting wind and the rattling lids, I heard the gritty thumping of her booted feet as she closed in on me. I couldn't even dodge without becoming a movie cliché and twisting my ankle. I reached the elbow of the alley just as she thumped into me from behind.

Alex coiled her strong arms around me, one across my face, the other over my belly. She drove me against the wall, taking the actual impact with her arms. It was hard enough to kick the breath from my lungs but not to break anything. As if she wanted to stop me without hurting me.

I was stunned more by my own panic than by the pounding. My eyes were rolling like a half-eaten deer's. The only thing I could focus on was the sibilance of Alex's breath across my ear as she spoke.

"You think you're pretty hot shit, don't you, sweetie?"

My mouth was bent out of shape against her leather sleeve, and the hard arm inside it. I tried to protest, but nothing I said came out clearly. She moved her arm down to my throat but before I could talk she spat out another comment.

"You tease me every time we clash, little Poppy Speeds. What's the deal?"

I could barely speak. "N–no deal. It's just, you know...mind games. Just for the show."

"I'm not talking about on the track. I mean the looks you give me. How you always warm up right in front of me."

"I...didn't mean to."

"Bullshit." She tightened her arm around my neck as she spat out the word. "Don't let the arms fool you. I'm not a guy. I don't need flashing lights and a map to see what you're doing."

"Wh–what am I doing?"

"You're a little curious. *What's it like with a woman? Would I like it?*"

"Um...I have a *boyfriend*."

"And if he was all you needed, then you wouldn't be flashing that tight little ass at me, now...would you?"

"I–I don't—"

"Yeah, you do. And trust me, sweetie..." She pressed her mouth so close to my ear she was practically inside me. "With me, you *won't* like it. You'll fucking *love* it."

"Ohh..." *Damn.* I mean, I was straight, of course. But in that moment, I truly believed her. "B–but I..."

"Save it, sweetie. I eat little girls like you for breakfast."

As if to prove her point, she sank her teeth into my earlobe. I squirted out a girly squeal which slowly changed shape and tone as she drew more and more of my ear into her mouth. I whimpered, as taboo desire dripped down from my heart to my belly...and below.

When she let my ear slip wetly from her mouth, her voice lost its sharp edge and took on a fuzzy depth.

"I think it's time you learned to...play nice."

The heat of her body on my back was a sharp counterpoint to the cold bricks pressing against my front. I was trapped by her size and strength.

She took her arm from around my throat, but only so she could tangle her fingers in my hair and pull my head back.

I was as vulnerable as I'd ever been, but the fear pumping through me was nothing compared to my arousal. She sank her teeth into the side of my neck and sliced another moan from my chest.

I found it near impossible to breathe, trapped between a hard body and an even harder wall. On the track, I was loud, and strong, and ready for a scrap. I was a terrier.

Here in the real world, I was simply terrified. Powerless and small and oh-so-soft. Mostly, being feminine was what I loved. At that moment, a little extra size and strength might have been useful, though.

When Alex slipped her hand off my hip and nudged it in toward my pussy, I froze in place. Was I really going to let her do this? Could I stop her, even if I wanted to?

The fabric of my skirt felt like scant protection against the strength of her fingers. Then she dipped her hand past it, to my bare thigh, and glided upward.

It was all too much, and I slapped my hand down on top of hers, trying like hell to twist her away from me. Of course, she was too strong, but at least she stopped.

"All right. I'm not a monster. You say the word, sweetie, and this ends right now."

I thought I could remember the word she meant. I just didn't think my mouth could form that shape.

Rather than speak, I slipped my hand off hers and reached up to hook it around her neck.

Alex moaned with desire as she lifted my skirt and cupped my mound firmly through my panties.

"Mmm. These feel frilly and ridiculous."

"Th–they are."

"Good. Just the way I like 'em."

"Uh..."

She grazed my neck with her tongue as she made tight circles with her hand. My nerves buzzed like cola all through my body as I jerked against her firm touch, but she just held me still as if drawing the heat out of me.

Alex leaned on my back even more heavily, pressing my stiff, braless nipples into the bricks. As she drew her hand up to the waistband of my panties, she released my hair.

But when she drove her strong fingers down and pressed them to my clit, she clamped her other hand around my throat.

I was beyond caught. I was captivated. She was in complete control, regulating my breath by the tightness of her grip. Regulating my pleasure by the firmness of her touch.

"Sweetie is very, very wet."

"Y–yes, ma'am."

"Lift up your top."

I slid my hand down from her neck and obeyed her order, pulling my tight T-shirt up from the waist. She released my throat and eased her weight back far enough that I could get the thing past my tits, and then she swooped.

Alex took my breast in her hand like she'd caught it escaping, squeezing the soft flesh so hard it took away what little breath I had. She pinched my nipple in time with her strokes on my clit, and the shockwaves from both fired inward so fast they met in the middle.

"Yeah, sweetie. I told you you'd love it."

Alex took her hands away long enough to grasp my shoulders and spin me on the spot. She slammed me back against the bricks and dived at me, taking my nipple straight into the heat of her mouth.

I had my hands up like she'd arrested me, and truthfully, I wasn't sure what to do with them. But as she drew on my stiff flesh, and tickled at me with her agile tongue, my legs turned liquid. There was no choice for me but to take hold of her hair, just to steady myself.

Alex switched to my other nipple and I groaned with sheer desire. She brought her teeth into play, pinching my bud between them like she planned to take it home as a trophy. The pain added such a spicy flavor to the ecstasy.

I fisted her lush hair as she moaned against my tits. She worked her way from one side to the other and I turned my face to the sky to sob with pleasure.

Suddenly, she moved lower, the wet heat of her mouth moving relentlessly toward the wetter heat of my pussy.

Oh, god. Was I anything *like* ready to be eaten out by a woman? My head was unsure, but my slutty little slit just kept saying *yes, yes, yes.*

Alex pulled my hand out of her hair and stuffed my bunched-up skirt straight into my palm. I grabbed it automatically and held it out of the way.

"Those are fucking sweet little pink panties," she said, with a hungry grin. "It's a shame what's about to happen to them."

I had no idea what she meant, until she took them in her teeth and wrenched back, literally tearing them off me.

She let the ruined panties fall into her hand and then stuffed them into her jacket pocket. "Souvenir," she hummed.

"Those were my favorite ones," I said, my voice more of a liquid moan than the fiery hiss I'd been aiming for.

"And now they're *my* favorites." She shot me a little wink and then turned her attention to my wanton slit. "God damn, you're pretty."

The cool night air kissed my waxed bare lips lightly. When Alex moved in for her turn, though, she was anything but gentle.

She ground her tongue against my juiced-up slit, her moans becoming lioness growls in seconds. "Fuck you taste good, sweetie."

"I–I'm still sweaty from the match."

"And how. Mmm." She drove her face against me, gliding her tongue up inside my pussy as I struggled to remain standing. She butted at my clit with her teeth as she explored my depths.

I couldn't contain the squeals and moans she awoke within me. All I could do was look to the stars again and howl with need.

As my knees trembled and I started to drift down the wall, Alex cupped my ass and held me up. She tossed my leg over her shoulder and pushed in hard against my cunt, stretching me wide open.

She glided her hot mouth up to my clit and hauled my stiff bud inside, suckling on it like it was saving her life. I slammed my hands down onto her shoulders, pulling at her more to keep my balance than to direct her anywhere. She clearly knew where she was going, already.

Suddenly, she pressed her finger to my wet slit, and glided it up inside. A few twists later she added a second, and pumped in and out as she set up a rhythm of suck-and-release with her mouth on my clit.

I'd always thought Neil knew what he was doing down there, but Alex had him beat by a long shot. Her fingers were as nimble as they were strong, and her tongue was a work of art.

Already I felt the tingle of a climax, forming deep inside me. Out of nowhere, Alex pressed another magical finger up against me; this time to my ass, and I gasped in surprise. When she eased it inside me, I practically burst.

My orgasm erupted, and for a moment, I was Poppy Speeds again, my voice a siren in the night as I howled out in delight. Pulse after pulse of ecstasy poured through me until I was utterly awash with it.

Alex peppered my bare mound with kisses, always in a tight orbit around my slit. She still had her fingers inside me when she stood, her height causing me to fall back against the wall again just to look up at her.

The big, strong woman twisted her fingers inside my pussy, an evil grin crossing her pretty mouth as she glided them out.

"I think sweetie has learned her lesson."

"Oh?"

"You don't poke a bear unless you're prepared to be...*eaten*."

Alex pushed back from the wall, and turned away from me. She'd already taken a few steps before I realized that was it. As far as she was concerned we were done.

Yeah, well that didn't work for me. I took a second to channel my derby persona.

"You hold it right fucking there, bitch." I could barely believe that was my voice saying that.

Apparently, neither could Alex. She stopped, and half-glanced back over her shoulder. I kicked off my heels and fisted my tiny hands. "Where do you think you're going?"

"Sweetie, I'm going home to feed my kitty."

"I got something to feed your kitty right here."

I pushed off from the wall and ran straight at her broad back. The moment I leapt at her, she turned, and managed to catch me without falling. She cupped my ass and held me high.

"What the fuck are you doing, sweetie?"

I fisted her hair with both my hands, pulling her head back.

"Shut up."

I planted my mouth on hers, sampling the sweet mix of her tongue and my juices. She moaned against me and I felt easily as powerful as I did when I was on the track.

Of course, she was still twice my size, and the only thing stopping me from falling to the street. But I was in charge at that moment.

"Put me down."

As she lowered me, I released her hair and swept my hands down her body. Her tits were firm and buoyant, and much bigger than mine. I gave them each a tight squeeze on the way past, but my goal was somewhere lower. Somewhere darker.

I seized her steel belt buckle and worked it open.

"Sweetie, what are you playing at?"

"Didn't I say to shut the fuck up?" Holy crap. I *never* swore. Turns out, though, Poppy Speeds had the mouth of a sailor.

With her jeans open, I put all my weight into pushing them down. Alex gasped as she finally seemed to realize I was serious.

Her panties were far plainer than mine. White cotton briefs. As I got her jeans down past her hips, though, I noticed a tell-tale wet spot.

I doubted I had the strength to tear them off her, so I simply slid my hand down inside, through her soft blonde hair until I found her gushing wet slit.

"What's wrong, big girl? Not so powerful now?" I punctuated my words with pumps of my fingers, getting deeper and deeper inside her heat with every pulse.

"Uhhh…" She grabbed my wrist, but only to try and direct me.

"Oh, no you don't." I slapped her hand away and pinched her clit, causing a quake to run through her entire body.

"Damn, sweetie…"

As I circled her bud, pressing harder and harder, I squeezed her breast through her bra and T-shirt. Mimicking her earlier move on me, I pinched her tightly in both places at once.

Alex leaned forward, pressing her lips to the top of my head as her breath gushed in and out. Clearly, I had more skill than I'd imagined, as her voice grew dry, and her pussy grew wetter than ever.

A moment later, she seized my hair and pulled it, as she bellowed out a climax. Her hot breath washed down the back of my neck as a body-wide shudder ran through her.

When her breath came back under control, I slid my hand free of her panties and shoved her back hard enough that she actually stumbled.

"Fuck, sweetie. I didn't expect that."

I gave her a wink. "Big girl learned her lesson, huh? You don't eat me, bare, unless you're prepared to be…*poked.*"

She zipped up her jeans and fastened the belt. "You know I'm only gonna hit you harder than ever next time we play. Right?"

"Wouldn't have it any other way." I glided my fragrant fingers into my mouth and moaned. The only thing better than Alex's rich, spicy flavor, was her wide-eyed reaction.

"Damn, sweetie. You're a lot dirtier than I thought."

"Oh, and next time? Winner sits on the loser's face. Deal?"

Alex chuckled. "Deal. We both win either way."

THE END

The Copy Room

I HAVE A WEAKNESS. It's one I give in to any time I can, but which I try to keep private. In fact, it's a well-guarded secret from *everyone*. Everyone, that is, except Millicent.

The thing is, I *love* to submit. That's not my weakness, that's just my love. But I'm a bigger girl, both tall and thick, and the one thing that really gets me off is submitting to a tight little femme.

She doesn't have to be young, but it's nice. She doesn't have to be pretty, but I do kinda prefer it. Above all, though, she just has to be *petite*.

And it just so happened that Millicent ticked *all* the boxes. Not to mention she had a beautiful, crisp English accent.

So, yeah, the trouble with her was not that she *knew* my weakness. It's that she *was* my weakness.

And my boss.

***

I was already typing away when she swanned in, her crazy high stilettos *click-click-click*-ing on the polished concrete floor. Her sheer black stockings gave her perfect legs a delicious sheen, and as she walked, a tiny sliver of bare thigh flashed between the dark nylon and her frivolously short skirt.

If she wasn't my boss, I'd totally submit to her. And if I wasn't so hot for her, I'd probably hate her.

Maybe I did hate her. But more likely I hated myself for nothing more than how badly I wanted to fuck her.

She stepped up to the side of my desk and leaned on it, tapping her slender fingers with that expensive wedding band, and those long, perfectly-manicured nails just within my line of sight.

The gold ring with its inset diamonds was flashy and gorgeous, but it was always her nails that caught my eye. And as long and impractical as they were, still I always pictured her plunging those fingers deep into my cunt.

Her nails were like her heels; gorgeous to look at, but completely impractical.

"Hilary." She sounded like a member of the royal family, and that always had me picturing her as a teenager, indulging in shenanigans with the other girls in some hugely expensive boarding school.

I had to take a cleansing breath to ease my tension. "Yes, Millicent?"

She dumped a bunch of papers in front of me. "I need copies."

Just that. No details, no manners. But the sweet, cultured sound of her voice sent hot tingles down my spine.

"Yes, ma'am."

I stood, smoothing my skirt down around my wide hips as best I could. Even in flats, I towered over my beautiful boss. Her gorgeous face only reached as far as my big, round tits.

Millicent stood her ground, her sharp gray eyes hovering around my mouth, like bees around nectar. The sweet scent of her perfume tickled its way into my nose.

"Your blouse is too tight, Hilary."

"Yes, ma'am."

"And your skirt is too short."

We played this game, or one like it, most days. I didn't know what her goal was, really, but I still adored the attention.

As far as I could tell, she was happy in her marriage. Yet every day since I started working for her, Millicent had been giving me all kinds of signals.

I picked up the papers and straightened my back, coming to my full height. Millicent raised a single eyebrow in reaction.

Thing is, I could pick her up, and twirl her over my head. As easy as hot, wet pie. I could hold her down against the floor or up against the wall or tight against my body and there'd be nothing she could do about it.

But that really wasn't my thing, and she clearly knew it.

After a few moments staring each other down, I lowered my eyes, then turned and headed for the copy room. Everyone

I passed kept their heads bowed to their work, keeping themselves to themselves. As if I were a dead woman walking.

At the copy room, I shoved the papers into the slot and set the machine going. Only the first few copies had glided out when I heard the little clicking drumbeat of stilettos on concrete behind me. Then a tiny clunk as the door closed, and the clacking of the lock.

I dared not move, in case I messed up. Or woke up.

Click. Click. Click. Click.

Like a metronome.

Click. Click.

Then nothing but the growl of the copier, and the ragged pull of my breath.

"Turn around, Hilary."

I closed my eyes and obeyed. I was suddenly alone, in a locked room, with my ultimate girl crush. My belly tingled with the sweet concoction of danger, taboo and pure arousal.

"Look at me."

I sighed and opened my eyes. Millicent stood before me, her hands on her hips, her head kinked deliciously to the side.

"How dare you simply walk away like that."

"Ma'am?"

"Mistress."

I swallowed heavily. "S–sorry?"

"Call me mistress."

"Sorry, mistress. You asked for copies."

She stepped forward, stabbing her heel against the concrete like it was a knife, and stabbing her finger at my face. I had to clamp my thick thighs together just to stop my legs failing.

"Screw the sodding copies. What about your attire?"

"M–mistress?"

Even with her tiny frame, she took up my entire world at that moment. Her scent, her soft skin, her hot breath. And that voice.

"Your blouse." She took hold of my collar between thumb and finger, pulling it to the side, baring a little of my throat. Her eyes flashed for a second as she viewed my skin.

Millicent licked her lips before continuing. "I told you before, it's too tight. You little slut."

Hearing dirty words, filthy insults, in her refined accent, was such a thrill I thought I might faint. I held my breath, knowing that as soon as it came out, it would turn into a wet moan.

Millicent brought her other hand up and worked at my top button.

"It's definitely not work-appropriate. It shall have to come off."

My whole body quivered with desire as she worked her long-nailed fingers down my front, opening my blouse all the way.

"Remove it, you bawdy harlot."

I whimpered with need as I shed the garment, tossing it to the floor.

"Which brings me to your skirt. Turn around."

I obeyed immediately, and then felt her soft hands working open the button. When she drew the zipper down, she stepped back, her heels clickety-clicking on the floor.

"Take that slutty thing off."

Again, I did exactly as I was told, dropping the skirt and standing there in only my black bra and panties.

"Turn around, you wanton little hussy."

The moment I spun, she put her hand around my throat and dug those impractical nails into my skin. She leaned herself forward and pushed me until I slammed back against the filing cabinets.

"You're a shameless wench, Hilary. Why don't you just put flashing lights around it?"

"Around what, mistress?"

Millicent blinked like time had slowed, and trickled down to her knees, releasing my throat. She trailed her hand down between my tits and then seized my panties.

Pulling them aside, baring my pussy, she narrowed her eyes as she glared up at me. Barely a second later, my sexy boss ran her hot tongue up the length of my wet slit, her eyelids fluttering in reaction.

"Why, this tasty little cunt of yours."

Holy. Fucking. Hell. One swift lick, and I was already simmering. I couldn't tell if Millicent had a talented tongue, or if it was just that I'd fantasized for so long about this moment.

Then, as quickly as it began, it finished. She stood, letting my panties slap back against me.

Millicent turned on the spot, and I felt tears welling. I thought she was about to walk out on me. Instead, she marched across the room and sat in a chair.

The copier finished its run right at that moment, and the silence that filled the room seemed thicker than ever.

Millicent slid herself forward in the chair, as if in anticipation. Of what, I didn't dare guess.

She gently ran her immaculate hands down over her knees, and back up into her lap. "I don't ruin my stockings for anyone. Least of all a strumpet like you, Hilary." She cast her eyes up and down my near-naked body, the slightest hint of a smile curling her lips. "Strip."

My breath faltered, and I closed my eyes as I removed my shoes, bra and panties, standing before my boss—and fantasy woman—naked. And wet as hell.

"A natural blonde. That's rare."

"Yes, mistress."

"Look at me, you vulgar trollop."

I opened my eyes and focused in on her beautiful pouty mouth. What wonders might she be capable of with that delicate fleshy opening? A quiver of want squirmed through my body as I pictured all the ways she could subdue me with that weapon of mass seduction.

"Come over here."

"Yes, mistress."

With me being so tall, and her being so short; with me standing and her sitting...it was the perfect match. I walked forward, finishing up with one leg either side of the chair.

Millicent took a long draw of breath in through her nose. When she released it, there was the hint of a sigh.

"Smutty tart," she said, then leaned forward, planting her mouth on my lips. For a moment, she simply held herself still, letting her heat and mine meld.

Then a soft moan escaped her throat, and she opened wide, gushing her hot tongue over my slit.

I shuddered from head to toe like I was being punched by pixies. This perfect woman had me whirling in seconds, flicking at my clit with that magical tongue.

She slid her small hands up and cupped my ass, pulling me forward, driving my cunt harder against her face.

It was all I could do to simply stand. As she pulled more and more sensations from deep in my belly, I fell forward, grasping at the chair back as I pumped my hips forward.

Millicent squeezed my ass, those picture-perfect nails of hers scratching hard enough to break the skin. Scratches that would take days to heal. Scratches that would remind me of this moment, and which I'd be fingering every time I touched myself.

The harder she scratched, the more I leaned, until I had her chair up on two legs. She was close to overbalancing and it was only my strength holding her up.

Millicent slid her hands around to my thighs and gripped, taking some of her weight as I pumped my hips forward and back, coating her beautiful face with my wanton juices.

Still she devoured me, every ripple, every fold, every pore of my pussy. I'd never had a woman so completely envelop me in her lust.

The hard little bump of her wedding band scratched against the skin of my thigh, and that was all it took. Knowing she had a husband waiting at home while she had her tongue buried in my cunt was like erotic dynamite.

Millicent clearly read my face. I felt sure it wouldn't be hard to do. Mouth wide open, cheeks hot with blood, eyes squeezed closed.

She fired one hand up and squeezed my nipple, pinching my skin with those incredible nails, and it was the detonator.

My belly became a galaxy of tiny stars, all going supernova at once, firing bursts of pleasure into my veins and muscles. I ground myself over Millicent's perfect mouth, drowning her in the wet heat of my cunt. She barely made a noise. Just dirty smacking sounds as her lips left mine for a split second, only to gush back home against me.

I had her bent halfway to the floor, and I feared my strength would fail any second. Millicent simply dug her nails into my thighs, spiking at my skin hard enough I thought she'd probably draw blood. And I didn't mind at all. That would just be ten more mini-clits to finger.

When my pulsing core finally let up, I used the last of my strength to pull the chair down forward onto its four legs. Immediately, Millicent stood, pushing me back hard enough that I landed on my bare ass on the cold concrete floor.

My petite boss stepped forward, until the center of her skirt was right in my face.

"Down." The way her lips formed the word gave my spine a jolt. The gloss on her face was so naughty, I could almost taste it.

"Mistress?"

She leaned down and glared straight into my eyes. Her breath, so close to my face, felt like the draft from the wings of passing butterflies.

"Lie down."

Slowly I rolled myself down onto my side, then flat onto my back. The polished floor bit into my skin with its icy teeth, until I gradually warmed it.

My body felt heavier than usual but my head and heart were floating up with the false ceiling. Millicent's beautiful face blocked out the overhead light, eclipsing me like a heavenly body. Her jet-black hair splashed around her eyes, flying in front of them and then away, like frightened birds.

The movement of her hands drew my gaze. Slowly, she gathered the soft fabric of her navy skirt and bunched it up, lifting it inexorably toward her slender hips. The hems of her stockings peeked out, her suspenders nosing into the brightness of the room.

My gaze settled on the waxed-bare skin of her naked pussy. She inched forward until the pointy toes of her expensive shoes nudged at my armpits. She was all I could see. All I could dream.

Slowly, like honey dripping, she turned on the spot. The glistening skin of her lips winked at me as she lowered herself, bringing that sweet, tasty treat ever closer to my searching mouth.

Her muscle control was incredible. The closer she came, the slower she moved. The heat of her radiated out all over my face, but I couldn't quite reach her.

Slowly, achingly slowly, she lowered herself all the way. The silken smoothness of her lips pressed to mine and I drew her magnificent scent deep into my lungs. She grabbed my tits hard, maybe for balance, maybe just to hold them. I didn't mind either way. I just loved having them played with.

I probed my tongue into her and listened for any change in her breathing. I thought maybe it turned a little deeper, a little quicker, a touch more ragged. But it was hard to tell for sure when I was drinking so deeply from the delicious wonder of her pussy.

Everything had happened so quickly, I had no idea of the rules. Was I allowed to touch her? I figured it couldn't hurt to try, and I lightly caressed her ankles, just above those beautiful shoes.

"Hm." That was the only sound she made, and I couldn't tell if it was a *yes*, or a *no*, or a *never stop eating my pussy, you filthy little whore*.

I slid my hands up to her knees, and she made no other sound, so I kept going, exploring the tenderness of her outer thighs and coming home to rest with my hands on her pert ass.

As I flicked my tongue across her clit, I squeezed those soft cheeks, and she let out the first true sound of pleasure that I'd heard. A small whimper, followed by a sharp intake of breath. Then she released her skirt and it fell around my head, blocking off everything that wasn't Millicent.

I slid my hands inward and pushed her a little higher, just so I could seize her clit between my teeth. As I squeezed it, I pressed a finger to her puckered back door, and she sighed.

That was all I needed. I'd found a weakness in her. Millicent was definitely in charge, exactly as I wanted...but I had a tiny bit of brat power I could wield if I wanted.

As I glided the tip of my finger into her ass, I bathed her cunt with my tongue. Her rich, salty musk filled my senses like a night at the beach.

Millicent let a long, low moan escape as she rolled her hips above me, grinding that sweet, fragrant flower of hers against my face.

"Hilary...ahh..." She tensed above me and then let out a sharp sigh. "Oh, fuck these stockings."

She came down onto her knees and pressed her cunt heavily against my mouth. Before I knew what was happening, she drove her fingers down the still-juicy split of my pussy and pulled my leg toward her so she could sink her teeth into my lower thigh.

I pulled my hips up off the floor, begging without words for her to come down and take care of my wanton cunt again.

"You really are an indecent little slut...aren't you, Hilary?"

"Yes, mistress. I'm a filthy, naughty, perverted little whore, and I need a severe tongue-lashing."

"Less talking, more eating."

I clamped my mouth over her delicious pussy and waited. It took all of two seconds before Millicent ran the heat of her tongue down my inner thigh and dived on my sticky slit like it was caviar.

My dirty boss hooked her arms through my legs, pushing my knees toward my shoulders, bringing my cunt up to meet her mouth. When she grabbed my ass, she spiked her nails in, harder than ever.

God, I would have so fucking many reminders of this session, for at least a week to come. I knew myself well enough to know I might miss a few days of work. Just so I could stay home and touch my sore spots while I jilled myself off like a dervish.

As Millicent lashed my slit with her perfect tongue, I sucked on her clit like it was an oxygen supply. I twisted my finger in her pretty ass and she whimpered quietly.

Her hot breath washed down over my pussy, and my ass, and I knew for certain she was right on the edge. I released her cunt just long enough to say four quick words.

"Please, mistress. Spank me?"

Millicent let a tiny, birdlike moan seep from her throat, but it quickly became a feline growl. And as she gnawed my clit with her perfect teeth, she landed her hands on my thick ass cheeks, time after time, working that skin raw.

She might be married to a man, but she had the most incredible touch for women.

I pictured how red my ass would be, and it wiped my mind clear of all other thought. There was Millicent, and there was me. Mouth to cunt and cunt to mouth.

And a moment later, the whole world was fireworks. Millicent jerked bodily on top of me, as her climax punched through her elfin frame. I rolled and rocked beneath her, my curvy body more of an ocean for her to surf on.

After what felt like forever, and like a split-second, Millicent finally released my pussy and sat up, mashing herself into my greedy mouth one more time.

And then she stood, my lips parting from hers with a delicious smacking sound.

With barely even a wobble, Millicent strode toward the door, leaning back against it. Waiting for me to dress, I assumed.

I sat up, and she followed my every move with only her eyes, a small, hungry smile on her lips.

"That pretty blonde bush of yours, Hilary?"

"Yes, mistress?"

"I'm afraid that's also work-inappropriate. I want it waxed."

"Um…" Was she saying what I thought? That she wanted more of this? Of me? Because I was totally down with that. "Y–yes, mistress."

I worked the rest of my clothing on, picked up the almost-forgotten copies, and walked as best I could on shaky legs toward the door. Millicent didn't move, still blocking the exit with her sweet, petite frame.

She seized my collar and pulled me down, planting a sizzling wet kiss on my mouth. Her sweet whimpering moans were music to me, and I sang back in harmony.

She broke the kiss and pushed me back, her eyes holding a devilish spark and her cheeks flushing with excitement.

"You look even more dishy with your makeup smeared like that, darling."

I'd never heard her speak to anyone so nicely before, and it left me speechless.

Millicent trailed her fingers across the papers I held. "Perhaps we could...duplicate this little session sometime."

"Mistress?"

"My husband travels a lot for work," she said. "I'll let you know when. My address is on file."

My belly tingled with anticipation. "Oh...yes please, mistress."

THE END

Bad Bride-To-Be

KIMBERLY PICKED UP HER tequila, and I picked up mine. She yelled out a toast to her upcoming wedding, we downed our shots, and we winced like lightweights. The booze was great, but it always burned.

This was our last Saturday girls' night as two single chicks. Cherise and Kimberly, painting the town red, in the bar where we had our first legal drinks three years before.

Okay, so she wasn't *truly* single. She'd been engaged to Mitchell since forever, but he was a cool guy and had never stood between Kimberly and a fun night out.

But that was as an *engaged* couple. I had no idea if he'd turn into some control freak asshole once he got that ring on my best friend's finger.

If he did, though, then maybe he'd stop her from seeing me.

We'd been besties since grade school, but if he ever made her choose between me and the D...well, I knew Kimberly like a sister. I didn't like my chances in *that* showdown.

When I'd picked the bride-to-be up earlier on, Mitchell had pulled me aside and asked me to watch out for her. Make sure she didn't let any guys get too friendly.

He must have understood how significant this night was. Her last Saturday night before she married him.

Kimberly herself seemed unfocused, and I didn't think it was the effect of the booze. She gazed around the bar, swinging herself side to side on her stool in that way-short skirt. Letting those long, bare legs of hers work their magic. She had more than a few guys slamming into walls and tripping over nothing.

I waved my hand in front of her face. "What's the buzz, Kimba? You seem distracted."

She screwed up her nose in that super-cute way that always made me want to tickle her.

"Just thinking."

"Didn't the doctor warn you about that?"

"Ha ha. Cow." She grabbed her next shot and downed it, then coughed like a two-packs-a-day man. "Damn, that's good."

I poked her in the ribs. "Don't think you can get out of answering me. What's wrong?"

She smiled, but it was a pale imitation. "This is it, honey. Everything changes now."

"It doesn't have to."

"No. But it probably will."

This was going into territory I really didn't want to think about, so I grabbed my next shot, and she followed suit. "To never changing!"

We slammed them down quickly, and the tequila burned like it always did.

When she recovered, Kimberly nudged my shoulder. "Why don't you ever pick anyone up these days, honey?"

"Why would I do that? This is girls' night."

"Exactly. I mean, think of all the cock you could get with these girls." She cupped my big tits and clapped them together, sending the random dudes around us into overdrive.

She'd always been the touchy-feely type, so I didn't think much of it. At least, not right then.

Suddenly, Kimberly slid forward off her stool. "C'mon. I need the bathroom."

"Don't do anything I wouldn't do."

"Um, you're coming too."

She grabbed my hand and tugged, so I relented. Kimberly's the sweetest drunk I ever met. She was tipsy rather than wasted at this point, but I still had my promise to Mitchell ringing in my head. It was probably for the best if she took a little break.

We pushed through into the ladies' room and she went straight to the mirror, checking her makeup.

"I thought you needed to pee?"

"Nope."

I came up behind her and stood off to one side. She poked her tongue out at my reflection.

"Once a goofball, always a goofball, huh?"

She pulled out her lipstick and winked at me. "You love it, honey."

She was right. I adored her free spirit and her dorky personality. I hoped she never lost those, no matter what.

With a slight feeling of melancholy, I put my arms around Kimberly's waist and leaned my head on her shoulder. "I'll miss this. Y'know, if we stop doing it."

"Then we'll never stop doing it, honey." She slid one hand over mine and squeezed.

"I don't know. You'll marry Mitchell, and before you know it, you'll start popping out rugrats. Meantime, I'll still be out here alone, drinking shots and luring hot guys to their orgasm, night after night."

She rolled her eyes as she applied her lipstick. "Such torture for you. And them."

I tightened my grip on her, as if it would stop things changing. "I don't want us to drift apart, Kimba. And that happens when husbands come along."

"Not Mitchell, honey. You know he's chill."

"He's not *that* chill."

She worked herself free of my arms and turned around, a slight furrow in her brow. "What do you mean?"

Fuck. I wasn't supposed to say anything about the promise. But I also could never lie to Kimberly. "He, um...asked me to watch out for you tonight. Make sure you didn't pick up some random guy and...y'know. *Go out with a bang."*

"Really? Did he think I'd just jump on the nearest cock and ride off into the sunset?"

I took her hands and massaged the backs of them with my thumbs. "I don't know what he thought. Maybe he understands this is a big night for us."

"Hmm." She sat back against the bench, and I knew right away there was something inside her. Something she needed to tell me.

"C'mon, Kimba. Spill."

"What?"

"I know you better even than Mitchell does. What is it?"

She eased her hands out from mine and slid up to sit next to the hand basin. Her incredible legs practically glowed in the low bathroom light. I thought nothing of it when she reached over and threaded her fingers into my hair.

"I've been...having fantasies."

"Of course you have, Kimba. It's normal and healthy and you're a whore."

"Bitch." She blessed me with her gorgeous smile and gave my hair a little pull. "I'm just worried."

"Why? You and Mitchell are sickeningly good together."

"Then why am I so scared? Why have my fantasies become so fucking strong in just the last few weeks?"

"I don't know. Is it one of those faceless dude fantasies? Sex with a stranger?"

She smiled as she shook her head. "Oh, it's definitely not that. This person has a face, and a fucking amazing body. And I so much want to act on it before it's too late."

"I told you my promise to Mitchell, right?"

She tugged my hair again, and the skin on my neck tingled to life. "Where are your loyalties, you cow? You're supposed to be on *my* side."

"I am."

"Besides, you wouldn't have to break that promise."

I frowned deeply as I stared into my best friend's eyes. "I don't understand."

"You said he wants you to keep me from fucking a random guy, right?"

"Right."

"Well, my fantasy fuck is not a random." She fisted her hand in my hair, and smiled. "And it's not a guy."

Before I understood what was happening, she pulled me forward, claiming my mouth in a wet kiss that sent sharp bolts of lightning down my spine.

I was mindless for a moment, parting my lips and drawing her sweet tongue inside me, my voice gushing out in a warm murmur.

Right up until I realized exactly what was happening, and my belly tightened in fear.

I pushed Kimberly back and stared at her, touching my fingers to my wet lips.

"Fuck. What was that?"

"Oh, come on, Cherise. You've been kissed before."

"Not by you." And never like that. Like she was the tide; drawing me forward, forcing me back, with a power that was impossible to resist.

Kimberly shrugged. "What can I say? I really want to fuck you, honey."

"I'm your fantasy?"

"Hell, yeah. God, you're so sexy it hurts me, sometimes."

Heat filled my cheeks. No guy had ever complimented me like that. With such raw honesty. "I can't believe it."

Kimberly reached over and took my hands in hers. "And *I* can't help it, honey. Even when I'm fucking Mitchell, all I can think about is you. I close my eyes, and everything he does, I picture it's you."

"Everything?"

"Okay, *almost* everything. When he kisses me, I pretend it's your mouth. Only..."

"Yeah?"

"Only now I've had the real thing." She explored my lips with her finger. "And it's so, so much better than the fantasy."

My eyelids fell closed of their own accord. I knew Kimberly as well as I knew myself. And in her voice, I could hear it. This was her absolute truth.

I opened slightly and flicked at her finger with my tongue. Kimberly sighed and pressed harder, roughing my lips up against my teeth, spreading them until she could guide that finger inside me.

I closed around her and suckled. It really didn't matter that this should never happen. I could feel it inside me that it was a done deal anyway.

I was about to fuck my best friend.

As I drew harder on her slender finger, Kimberly leaned forward and drove her teeth into the side of my neck. My whole back ignited in goose flesh, and I whimpered with the desire she'd awoken within me.

I tried to say her name but with her finger deep inside me, all that came out was a moaning sound.

Her only reply was a growl that vibrated against my skin as she tightened her hand in my hair.

The scent of her shampoo, and her perfume, and just her sexy, beautiful body, clouded my mind.

Kimberly slid off the bench and gripped my hair in both hands. She bent my head back and suckled on my throat. I closed my eyes and soaked up her attention, letting my voice escape in a long, juicy moan.

It was as if the earth moved beneath me, and for a moment I thought it was simply the weight of my desire shifting. Then the bathroom counter bounced against my butt and I realized she'd spun me on the spot.

Kimberly kissed a little trail from my throat to my chest, gliding her hands down my body. She slid them between me and the counter and gripped my ass, squeezing and lifting.

"Come on, honey. Up you get."

I worked myself up where Kimberly had been moments before. My bestie glided between my legs, and leaned forward.

Her kiss was far hungrier this time, and she growled with pure desire as she worked my mouth over. Her tongue was a force of nature as she plunged it in and out, like a little wet cock. She scratched her nails down the length of my back, hard enough I was sure she'd leave marks, even through my dress.

It was all I could do to stay sitting upright under the power of her attack. I swept my arms around her neck and held on, riding her motions like driftwood on the tide.

I'd never been with another woman, and hadn't ever given it much thought. And suddenly I realized I'd been missing out. Every kiss she gave me was like velvet-coated steel. Soft to the touch, but strong in the core. And impossible to resist.

Caught up in the moment, I wrapped my legs around her pretty ass and squeezed, pulling myself tighter against her.

It was nowhere near enough. Kimberly must have felt the same way, and she worked open my dress and my bra, never once breaking the hot seal of our mouths.

Only then did she step back for a moment, and only long enough to bare me from the waist up.

"Oh, god, Cherise."

I shivered under the intensity of my best friend's gaze, as she stared at every inch of my bare skin. My nipples peaked as if reaching out for her.

Kimberly dived straight at me, grabbing my boobs and squeezing while she latched her fiery hot mouth over my nipple. I swept my hands into her lush blonde hair and held on, pressing the soft weight of my tits against her beautiful face as she switched from one side to the other.

My best friend snarled at me like a tigress as she bit into my nipple, then slid her hands down to my knees.

She hummed out little groans of pleasure, her mouth still clamped to my stiff bud. I drove my hand down inside her tight top and found her breast, grabbing on and squeezing it like fruit.

When I seized her nipple between my finger and thumb, she whimpered. And when I pinched it tight, it was like everything changed for her.

She pushed back from me, so hard she stumbled across the bathroom, slamming her back into the wall. For a second I thought she'd come to her senses and was about to turn and flee.

But only for a second. Because that's when she made a playful growling sound and bounded across the room, falling to her knees before me.

She flipped my dress up and hooked her fingers into my panties, pulling them aside so sharply I heard the threads cry out in pain, and I gasped.

Hearing my shock, Kimberly glanced up. She knew me so well she must have read my mind. Or at least the arousal on my face.

She shot me a sly smile, which turned darker as she wrenched at my poor, doomed underwear.

A second later, she'd ripped them completely off me. I'd always known she had fierce passion, but who knew it could give her such strength?

"Ohh..." Her voice was somewhere between a hum and a hymn. She closed her eyes a moment and drew in a breath through her nose.

I caught my own scent in the air, and I tightened my belly, wondering if she'd stop then. Run away in fear. But when she smiled and gazed up into my eyes, all my fears evaporated.

"God, Cherise. You're so fucking beautiful."

She didn't even wait for me to reply. Just slid her hands under my knees and pushed up, overbalancing me back against the mirror. My ass slid forward a little, and it was as if I'd served my cunt straight to her.

Kimberly gouged her hot, wet tongue right through the juicy heart of my pussy, coming off just before she touched my clit. With her eyes closed, she drew her tongue back into her mouth and frowned, then licked her lips.

"You taste as fucking good as you look, honey."

My breath poured out in a long, sighing moan. Before it had finished, Kimberly pounced back on me, gliding her pretty pink tongue over my cunt, from side to side and top to bottom. Every pore of my pussy was soaking wet, from her mouth and my own juices.

I speared my fingers into her hair and hung on, grounding myself. As she dashed her sweet mouth against me, I curled my hips forward and back, gliding myself over her pretty face.

Kimberly swept her hands up my thighs, digging her nails in hard enough to scratch, firing my blood with bolts of danger, deeply entwined in fingers of bliss.

My bestie grabbed my inner thighs and pushed hard, spreading me wider than ever. She slid her fingers inward, then drew my lips apart and speared her tongue deep inside me.

"God, you're so fucking perfect, honey," she muttered between long, noisy licks.

I'd found heaven in a public bathroom. My best friend since grade school had her beautiful face buried in my cunt, and it was near perfect.

As if reading my mind, Kimberly ran the wide face of her tongue up my slit and clamped the wet heat of her mouth over my clit. Now it was *utterly* perfect.

She sucked on my pleasure bud like it was a thick shake, and pressed her thumb to my pussy. A second later, she plunged it inside me, and glided her finger across my puckered ass.

The eruption of bliss inside me was unstoppable, and only seconds later I fell screaming into the most tumultuous climax I'd ever had.

There was no doubt in my mind that everyone in the bar heard me, even over the music, but I simply didn't give a fuck. I had Kimberly's mouth on my pussy. That was all that mattered.

When the last wave of pleasure gushed through me, I curled my fingers around her hands and pulled.

"Come up here, Kimba."

She gave my pussy one last, lingering kiss, sending quivers of delight through me. As she rose, she made a long, meandering journey over my skin, kissing my belly and boobs on the way up.

Finally, I had her before me and I swooped on her, suckling my own arousal from her pretty, wet mouth.

Knowing she had to head back to Mitchell tonight, I couldn't treat her too roughly. So, I slid her shoulder straps down and eased her tight little boobs out of her top.

As I squeezed her stiff nipples, I licked my way up her cheek and nipped her earlobe. "Stay right the fuck there, Kimba."

She sighed at the obvious hunger in my voice, and I slid lower. As hard as I wanted to bite her buds, instead I simply latched on and gave each of them a pull with my mouth.

Even through her panties and past her skirt, her beautiful scent came up to kiss my senses. Just like mine in so many ways, yet not quite the same. Like two different bottles of the same wine.

I licked her soft belly as I slid to my knees before her. She sighed as I ground her slit through her skirt.

"That's so nice, honey. But not enough."

Though I wanted to rip her panties off with my teeth, instead I eased them down her sexy legs until she could step out of them.

Suddenly, there was nothing between my mouth and my best friend's cunt except a few inches of space.

"Fuck, you're pretty, Kimba." I glided my thumb up her slit and onto the waxed-bare skin of her mound. Her pussy was as wet as my mouth, and her juices coated my skin.

I glanced up at my best friend as I slid that thumb into my mouth and sampled her for the first time. The sharp, smoky flavor of her arousal burst against my tongue, and I knew right away I wanted more.

I wanted it all.

Kimberly gazed down at me, and I edged closer to her sweet cunt. She gripped the counter as she leaned on it, and then I closed my eyes and glided my tongue over the length and breadth of her pussy.

"Oh, fuck, honey. You've done this before."

"Uh-uh," I gasped out, between long, sucking pulls on her juicy lips. "First time."

I grabbed her tight ass and squeezed, pulling her toward me. When I felt her hard little clit against my tongue I growled and seized it, squeezing it between my teeth.

The sound of her moans was a symphony to me. More than anything, though, I wanted to see how I affected her.

I slid through her legs and lifted her skirt at the back, baring her gorgeous ass to me. From there, I could look into the bathroom mirror and see Kimberly's sexy face.

With a sly smile, I sank my teeth gently into the cheek of her ass, and she gasped and flashed her eyes. I made a big show of sucking two fingers into my mouth, and then tickled at her lips with them.

Kimberly slid one slender leg up on to the bench beside her. "Please, honey. Now?"

The need in her voice was everything, and I jammed my hand forward, driving those two fingers deep inside Kimberly's cunt.

All I was doing was what I'd do to myself, and I'd never felt more powerful. More in control. Because every twist, every thrust, every tiny hooking motion I made, reflected on her gorgeous face.

The spicy marine scent of Kimberly's pussy rose to meet me again, and I took a deep breath, filling myself with her.

It was too much to resist, and I trickled back down to my knees, gliding my lips across the silken skin of her inner thigh as I passed.

With my fingers still pumping, I clamped my mouth back over her cheeky clit and hauled on it as hard as I could. Kimberly let a long, low moan gush from her throat as she fell forward.

I hooked my fingers and pressed at her special spot inside. As I bit down on her clit, I stroked another finger over her puckered back hole and her whole body pulsed.

Barely a moment passed before she squeezed my fingers so hard I thought they might burst. When she released them, she let a high, keening wail of ultimate bliss fly from her throat, as she trembled above me.

I eased my fingers out from her pussy and lapped at her, drawing in every last drop of flavor. I wanted to remember every moment, every scent, every taste, just in case.

Kimberly eased down to her knees and put her arms around me. Her kiss was far gentler this time, but no less deep.

I rested my head on her shoulder, wishing we'd discovered each other like this before now. This time next week, she'd be a married woman.

"You okay, Cherise?"

"Yeah," I sighed, all the while meaning no.

"C'mon, honey. Spill."

I swallowed and kissed her again. "Everything I was scared of before? That we'd lose our girls' nights?" I shook my head at my own shortsighted fear. "That's nothing now."

"Why, honey?"

I cupped her face in my hands. "Because now? I won't be able to even look at you without wanting to fuck you. Like, ever."

She smiled and lightly shook her head. "That works for me."

"And Mitchell?"

"Trust me," she said with a wink. "He won't mind."

THE END

My Girl Crush

UNLIKE MOST COLLEGE GIRLS—AT least, the ones I know—I basically never go to parties. They're just not my thing, really. There's always too many people there, and none of them are *my* people. I'm not sure I even *have* people.

That's probably why they call me Leighton the Loser. Bitch Squad, that is. Tracey, Amanda, Shayla, Stacey and Jennifer. The ones who can't see past their own inflated lips, permanently held in duck-face pose.

But I was here at a party now, and for one reason only. It was being held by the engineering students. And that's the subject my girl crush was taking.

I could scarcely believe those words could go together in my mind. *Girl* and *crush*. As far as I knew, I'd always been straight. But there it was. I had a crush on another girl, and it was eating at me...in kinda the same way I pictured *her* eating at me.

Of course, all of Bitch Squad was at the party, too. Those chicks never missed a chance to take new pics to share online. Between them, they had more followers than Texas had cows.

And, as always, they'd dressed to slay. I'd dressed in my usual fashion, which is to say, totally out of fashion.

Short shorts to make my legs seem longer. Loose black T to play down the size of my tits. And a black beanie so I didn't need to fuck with my hair, because who has time?

And all of that so I could stay in the shadows, and on the fringe. If anyone tried to engage me in conversation it wouldn't be pretty. I don't *people* well. I'd rather be in my PJs watching cheesy sci-fi than surrounded by loud drunks screaming "woo" every two minutes.

But I knew my girl crush would be here. I didn't even know her name. She swaggered around campus like she was packing either heat, or meat. Always cool as an iceberg. Like she neither gave a shit, nor took any shit. A permanent sneer on her blood-red lips, no matter what.

The one day she wore a sleeveless top, I practically followed her around campus like a lost puppy. The girl has serious ink, over both arms. And it creeps inside up top, making me wonder how much more there was to see. And if she'd ever let me see it.

Some of the rumor-mongers said she was frigid. Others claimed she was a domme who pegged guys for money. But the ones I most wanted to believe claimed she was definitely into girls. Like I said, I never had been before, but for her I'd turn like a roulette wheel.

I finally spotted her, over on one of the black sofas. Normally she was in loose jeans and a leather jacket, but tonight she'd gone a little retro. Black leather skirt, red top, and a hair band. All of it tighter than my grocery budget.

She was sitting alone, which was both perfect, and sheer hell. Perfect, because I didn't want anyone else to see me make a fool of myself. Hell, because I *really* didn't want *her* to see that.

But she was the only reason I was here instead of streaming *Firefly* for the seven millionth time. So, I stepped right out of my comfort zone and sat beside her.

She kept her attention focused across the room, where all the cool kids were gathered. Didn't even glance my way. Just took a long drink of amber-colored liquid from her glass.

The suspense was killing me, so I leaned over to talk to her.

"Hi. I'm Leighton."

She turned toward me, her sneer game as strong as ever. "I know who you are."

"Y-you do?"

"I see you around, making those pretty eyes at me. Too jittery to come and talk."

"Oh. Yeah, that's me."

"You could, though. I'm not *that* scary." She gave me a tiny wink. "I only bite strategically."

My entire core tightened, as much from hearing her rich, smoky voice as from the words she said. It wasn't the first time I'd heard her speak, but it was the first time it had been to me.

Still, it was kind of embarrassing. I didn't know I'd been mooning over her so damn obviously. It wasn't like we crossed paths all that much, with her being an engineer and me doing commercial art.

"Um..." She still hadn't told me her name, but now I was too chickenshit to ask it.

A burst of loud cheering from the middle of the room interrupted whatever else I might have said. Which was cool, since my words had all dried up anyway.

I turned toward the noise. Through gaps in the throng of assholes, I could see two of the Bitch Squad girls dancing together. Tracey and Stacey. They weren't related but they looked like twins. Hair color from the same bottle, tits by the same surgeon, spray tans the same radioactive shade of nectarine.

My crush let a small chuckle burst out, just as Stacey planted a tiny kiss on Tracey's cheek. The small crowd gave a cheer and both girls raised their arms and shimmied. When they bumped their asses together, another burst of whooping erupted.

Both girls were very pretty and all, but the whole act was so cold and clinical. Nobody would ever believe either of them could be into anything but big jock guys.

"Some girls..." My crush shook her head and took another sip of her drink.

"I know." God, I sounded like a sycophant to my own ears. "Lipstick lesbian chic is so 90s."

My crush chuckled again, and my belly ignited. "Yeah, they're pretty. But they're straighter than my slipstick."

"Your..." I swallowed, as that word painted dirty pictures in my head. "Your *slipstick?*"

"Slide rule. It's kinda retro these days, but I like the old ways."

"I don't have the slightest idea what you're talking about." But I loved hearing her talk.

"Never mind." She gave me the slightest smile, then turned her attention back to the Stacey and Tracey show.

The girls came together for a little chaste kiss on the lips, and the guys went wild. It seriously was nothing more than a tiny graze of mouth against mouth, but everyone simply went apeshit.

"Yeah," I replied. "They're pretty, for sure, but...I mean, you'd have to *force* me to do that sort of thing."

She took another drink and laughed. "You'd be surprised how good it can be, miss Leighton."

That was, in my mind, the perfect cue. I leaned over and curled my hands around her arm, pushing my mouth up against her ear. "I'm sure it is. But like I said...*you* would have to *force* me."

My crush paused for a second before turning to me. "Well, well. What's a straight girl like you doing in a face like this?" She hooked her thumb back, indicating herself. All I could focus on was the deep crimson of her lips.

"I mean it. You'd have to grab me tight by my hair." I pulled my beanie off and shook my head, letting my long mane fan out. My crush watched closely, with lightning firing through her eyes.

I scooped up my hair and held it tight in a makeshift pony tail. "Like this. I mean, that's absolutely the *only* way you could force *me* to put my mouth on your pussy."

My crush raised one eyebrow, and licked her pretty lips. "Miss Leighton should not start something with me unless she's prepared for it to go all the way."

I slid down to my knees before her, my mind already blanking out the other assholes around us. Still holding my hair, I bowed my head, offering it as a prize to my crush. "I mean, if you took hold of this, and pulled my face down between your legs..." I had to catch my breath for a second. The picture I was painting took my words away. "Then I would have no choice but to eat your hot little cunt. Would I?"

She chugged the rest of her drink in a second and dropped the glass on the floor. "That's exactly how I see it. Let go of your hair."

I obeyed immediately. Some more primate sounds erupted behind me. I could probably imagine what Stacey and Tracey were doing, but I seriously didn't want to. Because my crush took my hair in both hands and slowly parted her legs, and that was all that mattered.

She squeezed her hands into fists, igniting my scalp in sweet pain. "Lift my skirt, miss Leighton."

I touched her knees and worked my hands higher, taking the black leather with me as I glided up her gorgeous thighs.

Only seconds later, her sweet, bare pussy was on display to me. Bare of panties, and bare of hair. And with a beautiful fiery tattoo above it that clearly stretched up onto her belly.

"Ohh..." I didn't mean to sound quite so worshipful, but finding out she was going commando was somehow even more exciting. Like she'd known I'd be here...and be *down there*.

My crush pulled me forward, twisting her wrists to press my mouth to the tender skin of her inner thigh. I planted a wet kiss there and moaned as I caught the sweet, oceanic scent of her pussy.

"Good girl, miss Leighton."

Her praise was as hot as her body, and it sent tingles of desire through me.

My crush directed my face across to the other side, and I lapped at her skin, savoring the hot hiss of want that came from her throat.

"Miss Leighton is naughtier than I thought."

"Yes, mistress."

"Oh...I like that. And here I thought you were straight."

"I am, mistress. I told you...you *have* to force me." I closed my eyes and whispered. "Please."

Another loud cat-calling session burst out from the other side of the room. Maybe Tracey had tweaked Stacey's tits or something equally lame and showy.

Meantime, over here in the shadows, my girl crush was pulling my mouth inexorably toward the enticing wet heat of her cunt.

Every one of my senses was devoted entirely to her. All I could see was her glistening slit, framed by the two alabaster thighs that were muffling my hearing. Her skin kissed mine with unbearable softness, and her scent drove spikes of need into me.

And then, finally, I tasted her.

She fisted my hair even tighter just as I pressed my open mouth to her slick pussy.

"Ohh...yes."

Her voice had turned deeper, more gravelly, as if all the liquid in her body had gone elsewhere.

While the crowd was over there, devouring a watered-down show, I was over here, devouring a beautifully wet pussy.

I could only imagine what would happen if that crowd turned around to see my ass in the air, barely covered by my shorts, and with my face planted squarely between the beautiful thighs of the coolest chick on campus.

The idea of being caught like that made my own pussy tingle with desire. Not that I thought anyone would notice us. They were completely focused on the two social media divas doing their tease-the-boys act over there.

I slid my hands up the insides of my crush's thighs, bringing them together tightly around her juicy slit. When I pressed in, it puckered her cunt up to meet me and I dived in hard.

Until the first time I saw this woman, only a few months ago, I'd never even thought of getting down and dirty with a chick. But as the rich, salt-and-honey flavor of her gorgeous cunt flooded my mouth, I realized I'd been cheating myself.

My crush pulled my hair and I gasped with the sweet pain of it all. She slid her ass forward just a little and curled her long legs up over my back. Her sexy slit parted just that little more, moving beneath my tongue as if welcoming me in.

"My clit, please, miss Leighton."

"Mmm...yes mistress." The sound of my voice came back so tightly into my ears, bouncing off the tenderness of her flesh.

I slid my tongue up the beautifully rippled folds of her pussy, and nudged at her bud with the tip. Even over the whooping galoots and the background music, I heard the rushed hiss of her breath when I circled her detonator.

As I clamped my mouth tightly over her clit, I glided the tip of one finger down through her lips, soaking my skin with her tasty juices.

The heat and flavor and scent of her sweet cunt filled me, and the last thing I wanted to do was take my mouth off her. But more than anything, I'd sunk myself into this little slave girl role, and I needed to ask for directions.

It wasn't so much that I didn't know what to do. I could touch her, lick her, suck her, exactly the way I'd like it and I was certain it would work for her. But this game depended on her being in control, and me obeying without question.

So, I stared up at her as I sucked hard on her tight little bud. Asking with my eyes the question I couldn't speak, because I was too busy eating her fucking perfect cunt.

"One finger, miss Leighton."

I sighed in relief, and closed my eyes to soak up the moment. Feeling bolder than ever, I secured her pleasure bud in my teeth and squeezed, as I drove one finger deep into my girl crush's pussy.

"Yesss..." She bucked against me, and I knew I'd done everything right. Then she crossed her ankles behind me and pulled with her legs, forcing my face to mash into her soft, slick flesh.

God, I'd never been so turned on. I literally had never wanted a woman before I'd seen her. Now, here I was, my mouth pressed so hard against her cunt that I could barely tell where my lips ended and hers began.

And all while, two dozen people—people we both knew—were in the room with us.

My own clit whined desperately for attention, and I wished I'd worn a skirt. I worked my free hand down and fumbled with the button and zipper on my shorts, finally getting them open and slipping my hand inside my soaked panties.

"Another finger, miss Leighton."

I glided my finger out of her and made a show of sucking her juices from it. A new fire lit in her eyes as she watched me, and I plunged a second finger into my mouth.

Barely had I pulled them back out than she dragged on my hair, slamming my mouth back into her cunt. I whimpered with the overwhelming pleasure of the moment and drove my two fingers inside her, just as I curled two more inside myself. It was like a filthy ballet. Synchronized frigging.

I pinched at my cheeky bud as I lapped at hers, my moans growing higher and faster as a sweet and spiky pressure built inside me.

"Are you playing with yourself, miss Leighton?"

I nodded, still refusing to give up my tasty treat.

"Bring those fingers up here."

My moans were from frustration as much as pleasure. I'd been getting myself going so nicely. But I was deep into this role, so had to obey.

Still pumping in and out of her searing hot slit, I slid my fingers out of myself and reached up to her, catching the slightest trace of my own scent on the way through.

My crush still had her fists in my hair, so she leaned forward, opening her fucking beautiful mouth slightly as she neared my wet fingers.

She kissed the side of them, closing her eyes as she drew in the scent of my arousal. Slow, like syrup pouring, she slid her tongue out and licked her way to the tips of them, like a porn star giving a blow job.

With one final little flick, she opened wide and slid her mouth down the length of my fingers, frowning with desire.

Her moan was too soft and deep for me to hear, but the sound of it vibrated against my skin. She slid her hot tongue between the two fingers and sucked and lapped at them, drawing in every trace of me.

I bit down on her clit again, and hooked my fingers inside her. She arched her back with need, her heels digging into my spine as she squeezed me all to hell and back. It truly didn't matter if it hurt. I wasn't letting up until this woman came against my mouth.

She pumped her hips harder, grinding her perfect cunt against my lips, and tongue, and teeth, and squeezing the hell out of my fingers.

And then, she bucked like a wild horse, and let out a long, slow moan of pure, distilled ecstasy, still muffled by my fingers in her mouth.

With her final pulses of pleasure, she fell back against the sofa, pulling her mouth off my fingers as she gasped for air.

She gazed down at me where I knelt, still sucking gently on her spicy cunt.

"Y'know, I'm gonna need to taste myself on your pretty mouth, miss Leighton. Come up here."

I came up, stumbling as I moved, clumsy as ever, to meet her waiting kiss. She slid her arms around my back as she slammed her mouth into mine and drove her tongue inside me.

The softness of her skin belied the strength of her kiss, and she licked at my lips like I'd licked at her pussy.

"Mm," she hummed. "I taste good on you, girl."

"Yes, mist—"

The rest of my words were cut off by another kiss, harder than before, and so taboo and erotic I thought my panties might just slide straight off me.

Just as suddenly, she broke the kiss and grabbed my breast through my T-shirt, pulling upward on it.

"And now," she said. "I need to taste *you*, miss Leighton."

"Ohh..."

"Up."

I stood slowly, my feet either side of her on the sofa. She kept her eyes spearing into mine as I rose higher and higher, and then let her attention wander south.

She grabbed my shorts and tugged at them, just bringing them past my hips. Her eyes flashed when she saw my panties.

"So wet," she said, her voice a purr that barely carried over the noise in the room.

"All for you, mistress."

"You're damn right it is."

My crush hooked my panties to the side, baring my pussy. She bit into her bottom lip as she studied me, the room's hot air feeling cold as it kissed my wet lips.

"Well, damn," my crush murmured, then straightened her back. She pressed her sweet mouth to my pussy lips and hauled in a long breath through her nose. "Double damn. You're a fucking delight, miss Leighton."

"Th–thank you, mistress."

She stole every other word and thought at that moment, opening her mouth wide and gliding the heat of her tongue up my slit. I had to throw my hands against the wall to keep my balance, though every long, fast lash of her tongue threatened to cut my legs out from under me.

I'd been kissed down there before. Licked. Bitten sweetly. But never by anyone with the skill of this woman. She had me on the verge of collapse within seconds, yet bizarrely I felt as if I were hovering in the clouds.

When she pulled my clit into her mouth and bit down, I let out a sharp wail of need. I couldn't believe nobody had noticed us. All still caught up in the fake show over yonder, and missing the real action here on the sofa.

The taboo sensation of what I was doing—having sex with another woman, in a public place—worked delightful fingers of pleasure through my body. I pumped my hips against my crush's lips, and she snarled and growled as she sucked on my tender flesh.

Working quickly, she plunged two fingers into her mouth, then drove them up inside me. I scratched so hard at the wall I swore I left marks.

When she worked her thumb onto my clit and made hard little circles, I knew it was all over and done. The big ball of pressure inside me erupted into a starburst of pleasure. Spiked balls of ecstasy pumped out through my blood and bounced off bone and simply filled my head.

The last ripple of bliss coursed through my body, and I turned limp, sliding down to land in her lap, mouth-to-mouth with this fucking sexy woman.

More yelling and cat-calling burst forth from the crowd, and we broke our kiss to look across there. Stacey stood behind Tracey, and had her hands on the other woman's tits. Both still fully clothed.

My crush chuckled again. "All those boys getting hard for a softcore performance."

"Uh-huh."

She sank her teeth into my earlobe, awakening a fresh tingle of desire down the length of my back. "Speaking of performances, I want a repeat one with you."

"Ohh...yes, mistress."

"Tonight."

I stood so quickly, my shorts almost fell down. I hurriedly zipped them up as my crush stood. She was much taller than I'd realized, which only made her even cooler to me.

"Can...can I confess something, mistress?"

"Of course, miss Leighton."

"I don't know your name."

"That's cool. If I told you, you'd only end up tattooing it on your ass. Just keep calling me mistress."

THE END

My Punishment

THE GIRLS' BATHROOM WAS quiet, and the lights were off, but that didn't mean we were safe. The damn nuns patrolled the hallways like this boarding school was a jail.

"Delores, go check the hallway. Linda, check the stalls."

"Yes, Eliza," they chimed, in unison. These two were the closest I had to actual friends here. As far as I could tell, they kind of worshipped me. Probably because I was the first—and so far, only—girl in our year who'd turned 18.

The coast was clear, so I pulled out my pack of cigarettes, and lit three of them up. Linda looked at hers like it was a cockroach. Delores had a little more confidence, but still seemed out of her depth.

"Come on, ladies. Put 'em in your mouths and suck."

Linda, the youngest of us by almost nine months, sniggered at my choice of words. Delores simply rolled her eyes and looked at me for approval.

I took a long drag from my cigarette and held it in, fighting the urge to cough. These two didn't need to know this was my first time smoking, as well. I had a rep to think about.

My two minions followed suit, but immediately coughed up their smoke.

"Lame, ladies. So lame."

"Sorry, Eliza."

I was about to give them a little more hell, when suddenly, hell came calling. In the form of Sister Gretchen.

"What on earth are you doing, girls?"

Dolores and Linda immediately hid their cigarettes behind their backs. Like that was any use to them. I simply turned to face my enemy, taking another long haul on my smoke.

"Well?" This woman had been targeting me all year, ever since she arrived at the school. She had a real hard-on for enforcing the rules. I, on the other hand, had an unhealthy hunger for violating them.

"I don't know about these two," I said. "But I'm learning how to suck dick."

The bathroom went silent for a moment as the penguin bitch walked right up to me.

Delores spoke first. "We're sorry, Sister Gretchen."

"Put those horrible things out."

"Yes, Sister."

They threw their cigarettes into the toilet and flushed them away. The nun turned to me, fire and brimstone in her eyes.

"Miss Tweed?"

I blew my load of smoke into her face, rather than answer. My nun nemesis held her ground, her only reaction a slight raising of one eyebrow.

As I made to take another puff, the Sister took the cigarette from my hand and dropped it to the floor, extinguishing it with a foot that pounced out from beneath her habit, like a trapdoor spider.

Then she held out her hand. "Give me the pack."

I made sure to roll the hell out of my eyes as I handed over my cigarettes. Sister Gretchen slid her hand inside her habit, and when she brought it back out, the pack was gone.

"You got a secret compartment in there, Sis?"

She held my gaze as she spoke, though her words were clearly for my so-called friends. "You two. Back to your rooms."

"Yes, Sister."

"But this is your *final* warning. Stay away from this...troublemaker." She indicated me with a brief nod.

"Yes, Sister Gretchen."

My traitorous buddies scampered away, leaving me here with the bitch who'd been making life hell for me. I decided the best form of defense was attack.

"I'm not a troublemaker, y'know. I'm a trouble-*finder*."

My teacher gave me a derisive smirk. "Oh, I see. You're the Howard Carter of bad behavior, are you?"

"Howard Carter was the Howard Carter of bad behavior. I'm more like...the Amelia Earhart of *fun*."

The sister shook her head, as if my existence alone was enough to tire her out. "You irk me, girl."

"Woah. D'you kiss your Reverend Mother with that mouth?"

She waved away my baiting and continued. "You're clearly very intelligent. Most of your peers would have no clue who Howard Carter or even Amelia Earhart were. Yet you fritter away your talents with this kind of...stereotypical rebellion."

If I didn't know better, I'd swear this chick was trying to bond with me in some way. Maybe playing bad cop had failed so badly she was switching to good cop. It wouldn't work.

"Well, you only have to put up with me for a few more weeks, Gretchie-girl. Then I'm out of this school, and more importantly, out of this lame-ass town. For good."

Sister Gretchen furrowed her brow, then seized me by the arm. "Then I'd best make the most of the time I have left."

She dragged me out of the bathrooms and through the hallway to her office. Once inside, she closed the door and marched me to the center of the room.

"Stand there."

She stood before me, her face eerily calm. She was the only nun here tall enough to actually stand eye-to-eye with me. Up close like that, I was surprised to see she wasn't that old. 25 or 26, maybe a little older. Definitely not yet 30.

She crossed her arms and kinked her head slightly to the side. Waiting for me to break, and talk first.

In the low light of the room, her black habit practically disappeared. Framed by the white of her coif, her face looked as if it glowed with a holy light.

And as determined as I was to stay in control, somehow this young nun got through to me. It was impossible to treat her as just some faceless enemy, when all I could see was her face.

"Why do you keep picking on me?" I sounded petulant, even to myself.

"I *correct* you, because it's what you crave."

"Bullshit."

Again, her only reaction was the raising of a single eyebrow. But it worked like hell on me.

"Sorry, Sister Gretchen."

My enemy moved around behind me, becoming nothing more than a calm voice. "You're certain I don't understand you, Eliza, but I've read your records. Daddy shoved you into boarding school when mommy deserted you. *Boo hoo*. You think your situation gives you certain rights?"

"Ha. I can't believe you're trying to lecture me about my life, when you don't have one of your own."

"Be careful with your assumptions, you little slut."

Her voice came from so close behind me I jumped. Her tone was so cold it had my nipples spiking. And to hear her use a dirty word was...well, it was actually kind of exciting.

She appeared in front of me again, a floating face.

"I've known girls like you before..." The Sister cast her eyes to the side, a dreamy expression crossing her face for a few seconds, before she hardened up and turned back to me.

"You think your looks and your cherry-picked First World Problems make you unassailable. Yet all you really crave is attention." She reached out and lightly brushed my hair back over my shoulder. "Praise is your queen, but she's so demanding, isn't she? Condemnation is so much easier to come by."

I had to swallow heavily for a moment. It was like she'd read the fine print on the back of my mind. "Yeah? Well...fuck you."

"Fuck me? Oh, touché. You should write that one down, so you don't forget it." There was a sharp anger in her eyes this time, and she studied me from head to toe and back again.

"Your uniform is a mess, Miss Tweed. Is that ketchup on your blouse?"

"I got caught in the middle of a food fight earlier." *Which I started.*

"Remove it."

"Wh–what?"

"Remove your blouse. I won't have you looking slovenly in my office."

It was clear Sister Gretchen was serious about this. As much as I loved rebelling, all the fire had gone out of me when she flagellated my mind a minute ago.

I had to fight like hell against the trembling in my fingers as I unbuttoned. With my blouse open, I paused in hope, keeping my gaze on the floor. My tormentor cupped my chin and pulled my face up so she could look me in the eye.

"Off."

My only protest was a sharp narrowing of my eyes, and then I slipped the garment off as if this was nothing unusual.

The nasty nun flicked the shoulder strap of my hot pink bra. "This is about as far from dress code as can be."

"Yes, Sister Gretchen."

"Remove it."

"What? No!"

"Oh, dear." She moved across the room so smoothly in her floor-length habit, it was as if she'd hovered. I stared in shock when I saw what she took down from the shelf.

A paddle.

"Perhaps you need more incentive to obey."

The trembling in my hands had migrated and spread. Now it was my knees that threatened to falter. Yet it wasn't pure fear that filled me. I was suddenly horny as hell.

I fumbled with my bra clip, never once taking my eyes off the dark stained cherry-wood paddle as Sister Gretchen bounced it in her hand. When I removed the lacy garment, there was no way to hide the twin peaks of my arousal.

The Sister reached out with the paddle, pressing it lightly to the side of my face, then drawing it down around my throat, pressing the thin rounded edge deep into my skin.

She detoured into the valley between my breasts, then slid across to my nipple, holding the tool directly beneath my bud like a shelf.

"Do you see?" she asked me, her voice turning dry and dark.

"S—see what?"

"See how obedience becomes you." She brought the paddle back up, pressing it under my chin and easing my face to one side, and then the other. "Indeed. You've never looked quite so comely as you do right now, Miss Tweed."

I couldn't believe this was really happening. Sister Gretchen was making a *move* on me? I should be reporting her ass to the authorities.

Except...

Except *she* was the authority in this room, and I couldn't deny how much it turned me on to have her being so controlling.

She stroll-hovered around behind me again. "Your skirt is too short, Miss Tweed."

"Y—yes, Sister."

"You know the drill by now, of course."

When I didn't move, she stroked the paddle across the backs of my thighs.

"I take it by your hesitation that your underwear matches your bra?"

"Um...not exactly, Sister."

This time she tapped the paddle against the side of my thigh, hard enough to be a true warning. "Explain."

"M—my underwear matches...my breasts."

The only sound in the room at that point was my ragged breathing. And then the tap-tap-tap of the paddle against Sister Gretchen's palm.

"Remove your skirt, girl."

I clamped my eyes shut as I unbuttoned and unzipped. I kept them closed as I dropped the skirt to the floor, leaving me standing there in nothing but my white knee socks and black shoes.

She placed the paddle, edge-first, on my shoulder, and stroked it across to the other side. Like *she* was my queen, knighting me.

When she spoke again, her voice was low, and liquid. "I see you weren't lying this time, Miss Tweed. Though I'm not certain that counts as a virtue in this instance."

"No, Sister."

My attention was almost completely on the paddle, which she ran over my back, moving it lower in a meandering pattern.

"Assume the position, Eliza."

"Sister?"

She fisted my hair and drove me forward, bending me over her desk. I grasped at the edge of it as adrenaline pumped through me.

Still with her hand in my hair, tight as hell, she pressed the paddle to my bare ass. The cold kiss of the wood made me jump, even though it was barely a feather of a touch.

"Count for me, Miss Tweed."

"Excuse me?"

She pulled the paddle back and swung it against me, the cracking sound hitting my ears before the sting of impact truly registered. A split second later, my world turned to fireworks as sharp agony bloomed on my ass. I let out a squeal that was far too tiny and child-like to be anything like a true representation of my pain.

"Miss Tweed?"

I swallowed the lump of tension in my throat and gagged out a single word. "Sister?"

"Count the strokes, please."

I grimaced once more as the heat of the spank gradually eased. Tears welled in the corners of my eyes, and my nose was ready to join in as well.

"One," I murmured, my voice breaking a little even on such a short word.

She repeated the dose, on the other cheek. The pain was, if anything, worse this time. Not just because I'd expected it, but because it piggy-backed onto the first stroke.

"T–two..."

The woman kept a steady pace, landing stroke after stroke. I couldn't tell if she was striking my ass harder, but every single blow hurt more than the one before it. My skin burned like I'd been in the sun for hours.

My voice broke after the sixth, becoming nothing but a ragged whisper as I counted off my punishment.

Every impact washed through me like a tide, scraping my bare nipples over the desk top. I squeezed the edge of the wood as I tried to process the strange cocktail of pain and pleasure that simmered away inside me.

After a dozen blows, she paused. I jumped when she placed the paddle onto the desk beside my head.

"Stage one is complete," she said. "Good girl."

I bit my lip as her praise wormed its way inside my head. Not only was it totally unexpected, it struck me deeply. What was it she'd said before? *Praise is your queen.*

Well, damn her for somehow knowing me that fucking well. That spanking had hurt like hell, but here I was. I took that licking and I was still ticking.

"Miss Tweed? Have you anything to say?"

"Can I have my cigarettes back?"

Sister Gretchen made an odd humming sound. I'd expected anger, or disappointment, but it sounded more like fascination to me.

"Then stage two begins."

She took my hair in both hands and pulled on it, dragging me to a standing position, her body pressed tightly against my back. After the sharpness of my spanking, the pain in my scalp was little more than an attention-getter.

"Wh–what are you—"

"Silence."

She pulled down and back on my mane, overbalancing me against herself. She stepped back, still dragging down on me, until I landed on my bare ass on her floor.

Still she pulled my hair, until I was lying flat on my back. I crossed my hands over my bare pussy, as if that would somehow save my modesty at this point. All it truly did was push my breasts up toward her.

My dominator stepped over my prone form, one foot either side of my hips. The fabric of her habit felt rough where it draped over my skin.

And then, suddenly, it was gone. As I watched, Sister Gretchen hitched the thing up, stopping when it reached her knees.

"You have a smart mouth, Miss Tweed."

"Yes, Sister."

"It's time to find out what else it can do."

She drew her habit higher still, revealing long, shapely legs. She was much fitter, and more gorgeous, than I'd ever have thought.

As she raised the garment further, she lowered herself to her knees. And suddenly I understood exactly what was happening. What my punishment would be.

Although, I caught myself wondering if it truly would be punishment at this point. This woman had worked me up into a frenzy that was as much to do with my submission as it was my arousal.

Sister Gretchen inched forward, pulling her habit up that last few inches, and baring her hairless cunt to me.

Another surprise. I guess I'd assumed all nuns went all-natural.

I licked my lips out of nerves, but the naughty nun just smiled down at me.

"That's the spirit, girl."

A wave of her musky feminine scent washed over me, and I had a fresh burst of nerves. Could I really do it? I'd tasted myself, of course. You don't masturbate as often, and as furiously, as I do without licking your fingers at some point.

My thoughts evaporated mid-stream, as Sister Gretchen tucked her habit behind her thighs and planted her hot pussy on my mouth. Her face, still framed by her pure white coif, floated above me as she took hold of my hair in both hands again.

I parted my lips, and her rich flavor burst against my tongue. Salty and complex, her juices tasted similar to my own.

She fisted her hands, awakening my scalp from a brief slumber. I pulled her wet lips into my mouth and sucked hard on them, flicking at her flesh with the tip of my tongue.

Above me, looking down, my punisher kept her expression almost completely neutral. Tiny spasms erupted in random places, as if all her demons were trying to claw their way out through her face.

I let a small whimpering moan out and the Sister pulled on my hair.

"Silence...Miss Tweed. Or there will be...uhh...consequences." She kept her voice mostly steady, which I simply took as a challenge.

I parted my thighs and glided one hand down onto my own juicy lips, grinding in tight circles as I lapped at my teacher. My other hand I brought up, sliding it under her habit and over her hip until I could press it onto her clit.

That little move seemed to break her. The moment I ground at her bud, I pumped my tongue up inside her, and she let out a short, barking moan.

Sister Gretchen pumped her hips forward and back, coating my mouth and chin with her delicious juices. She pulled one hand from my hair and reached behind herself, grasping my breast and squeezing it like a grapefruit.

A long moan of pleasure erupted from deep within me, and I worked a finger inside myself. My disciplinarian tightened her fist in my hair as she pinched at my nipple, and it sent sparks flying through my blood.

"I said silence, girl. So, consequences it is," she said, a tiny lop-sided grin curling over her pretty mouth. She inched her hips forward, drawing her tasty cunt out of reach of my mouth. "My ass."

"Sister?"

"Lick it."

"Ohh…"

I snaked my tongue down between the roundness of her cheeks, finding the puckered hole within and pressing it. The Sister sighed and closed her eyes as I ran rings around her ass.

"Very good, Miss Tweed."

Again, the simple act of praising me hit me like a deliciously hard slap on the bottom. Pleasing this woman gave me more of a thrill than defying her ever had.

My teacher whimpered above me, then made a fierce snarling sound. She raised herself off me and whipped herself around until she faced my feet. Then she planted herself on my hungry mouth again.

I slid my hands up over her hips and grasped her tight ass, squeezing it hard as I drove my tongue back inside her. Sister Gretchen fell forward, taking my neatly-cropped cunt in her mouth and gnawing at it with her teeth and lips.

She worked a short-nailed finger deep inside me as she squeezed my clit between her teeth, and I squealed in ecstasy.

I hooked my knees up toward my shoulders, opening myself to this woman, inviting her to do anything she wanted to me. She glided her tongue down the length of my lips and pressed the tip of it to my ass. As she tickled that hole, she pinched my clit and I knew instantly I was too far gone to ever come back.

I tried fighting fire with fire, biting at Sister Gretchen's clit as I glided a finger inside her ass. It seemed to work, her voice turning from hiss to siren in seconds.

When the Sister drove her tongue inside my back hole, and two fingers in the front, I took the final stumbling steps over the edge of the cliff. I squeezed her clit between my teeth, hard as I dared, to make sure she came with me.

My orgasm burst inside, shooting lightning bolts through my bones and muscles. Sister Gretchen called out in ecstasy as she squeezed my finger to death.

Even when our climaxes eased, she still nuzzled her face in against my tender, wet lips, lightly kissing and licking at my sensitive flesh.

Finally, she rolled herself off me and stood, smoothing her habit down her body as if nothing had happened. If not for the glistening of my juices on her face I'd wonder if I'd dreamed the whole thing.

"Get dressed, Miss Tweed."

"Yes, Sister."

By the time I had my clothes back on, Sister Gretchen had sat behind her desk and pulled out a bible. She rolled her rosary beads through her fingers, much as she'd rolled my clit between them earlier.

"Will that be all, Sister Gretchen?"

"That depends." She glanced up from her reading. "Do you feel you've learned your lesson?"

"I don't know. But I've made a decision."

"And what is that, girl?"

I licked my lips and went for broke. "Well, I realize I only have a few weeks left here before I'm gone for good." I leaned on her desk and murmured to her. "And I plan to milk every moment of it, Sister Gretchen."

She raised that one eyebrow again. "I see. Then you should return to your dorm."

Just as I opened her office door, she called out. When I turned back, she tossed me my pack of cigarettes.

"And I think you're going to need these." She turned the page of her bible. "You know my roster for hall patrol."

My belly fluttered with excitement, as I pictured more and more possibilities with this woman.

"Yes, Sister."

THE END

I have more FF Erotica than you can poke a...stick at!

Sign up for my newsletter to keep your finger on my...pulse!

Find it all on my website: stephbrothers.com

About The Author

Steph Brothers likes it dirty and writes it that way. Stories with claws to scratch all your deepest, darkest and naughtiest itches.

Check out my website for more books and shenanigans.

stephbrothers.com

Printed in Great Britain
by Amazon